D0182255
SAN RAFAEL PUBLIC LIBRARY
1100 E Street
San Rafael, CA 94901
415-485-3323
srpubliclibrary.org

ADAPTED BY KATE HOWARD

SCHOLASTIC INC.

No part of this publication may be reproduced in whole or in part, stored in a retrieval system, or transmitted in any form or by any means, electronic, mechanical, photocopying, recording, or otherwise, without written permission of the publisher. For information regarding permission, write to Scholastic Inc., Attention: Permissions Department, 557 Broadway, New York, NY 10012.

ISBN 978-0-545-74639-7

LEGO, the LEGO logo, NINJAGO, the Brick and Knob configurations and the Minifigure are trademarks of the LEGO Group. © 2015 The LEGO Group. Produced by Scholastic Inc. under license from the LEGO Group. Published by Scholastic Inc. SCHOLASTIC and associated logos are trademarks and/or registered trademarks of Scholastic Inc.

10 9 8 7 6 5 4 3 2 1 15 16 17 18 19 20/0

Printed in the U.S.A. 40
First printing, March 2015

A TEAM DIVIDED

During the final, epic battle against the Overlord, Zane gave his life to save his team.

After losing their friend, the other ninja went their separate ways. Only Lloyd stayed behind to train with Sensei Wu and Sensei Garmadon. He was helping test the security Cyrus Borg had built for the Golden Armor.

"You got closer than I thought you would," Borg said.

"Where are the other ninja?" asked Sensei Wu.

"They, uh, wanted to be here, but they had other plans," Lloyd lied.

Sensei Wu shook his head. "The absence of Zane will either tear you four apart, or bring you closer together. The choice is yours."

Lloyd wanted to get the ninja back together.

First, he found Jay, who was hosting a television game show.

"The team needs you more than ever," Lloyd told Jay. "This isn't you. You're the Master of *Lightning*, not the Master of *Lighting*. You know where I'll be if you change your mind."

Next, Lloyd found Cole working as a lumberjack.

"The team needs you now more than ever," Lloyd told Cole.

"I'm tired of fighting, Lloyd. Out here, no one expects anything," Cole replied.

"If you change your mind, you know where I'll be," Lloyd said.

Finally, Lloyd found Kai, who was fighting in a secret club. "Kai, the team needs you now more than ever," Lloyd said.

Kai shook his head. "Who says the great and powerful Green Ninja needs a team? You're doing fine on your own."

"I get it, Kai," said Lloyd. "You've run out of bad guys to fight. But when are you gonna start thinking of someone besides yourself?"

A NEW NINJA?

A few days later, Lloyd got his wish. The four ninja agreed to meet at Master Chen's Noodle House.

Kai reached for some noodles, but Lloyd stopped him. "Talk first, then eat."

"I'm hungry. Make it quick," said Kai.

"Without Zane, things have been different. But we have to move on," Lloyd began.

"Maybe we should add someone new to our team," Lloyd went on.

"A new ninja?!" blurted out Kai.

"Zane is irreplaceable," said Cole.

Lloyd frowned. "I cared for Zane, too, but now it's time to care about this team."

"Without Zane, there is no team," said Kai.

Suddenly, three thugs stormed into the noodle shop.

"Here comes trouble," warned Jay.

Kai shook his head. "They aren't our problem. We can't save everyone."

Then a thug blocked the food on its way to the ninja's table.

"All right," said Cole. "Now they're our problem."

Cole approached the thugs. "Excuse me, it's not polite to touch someone else's food."

"You better listen to him," said Kai. "He's no fun when he's hangry."

One of the thugs slammed a rice ball against Cole's chest.

"Was that really necessary?" Jay sighed.

As the ninja fought side by side, Lloyd asked, "How can you walk away from this?"

"All right, I admit it," said Kai. "We make a good team."

Cole took a bite of food as it flew through the air. "Everything's better on a full stomach!"

After a few minutes, it was clear the ninja were unbeatable. The thugs fled.

THE INVITATION

The ninja chased the thugs out the back door. They had disappeared, but there was a poster hanging in the back alley.

"It's Zane," gasped Kai.

"This poster says he's alive!" cried Lloyd.

"Those thugs weren't delivering a message to the Noodle House," Kai said slowly. "They were delivering a message to us!"

Lloyd pointed at the table in front of them. "Look!"

"Fortune cookies?" Jay said.

Jay, Kai, and Lloyd carefully cracked the cookies open. But not Cole. He popped the whole thing into his mouth.

"You do realize there's a fortune inside?" asked Kai.

"So that's why they're called that!" said Cole.

Lloyd read his fortune. “Listen to this: ‘Master Chen has invited you to participate in his Tournament of Elements—’”

“Master Chen?” Cole gasped. “Like, the-man-who-fills-my-belly-with-delicious-goodness Master Chen?”

Kai nodded. “‘Secrecy is of utmost importance. Tell no one, or suffer the consequences . . .’”

“‘If you ever want to see your friend again, meet on the pier at midnight and leave your weapons behind,’” Jay read.

Poof! Jay’s fortune fizzled and disappeared. Kai’s and Lloyd’s did the same.

Cole’s belly rumbled. He burped up a cloud of smoke. “Ouch! Well, at least I know I was invited.”

"It could be a trap to lure us in," said Kai.

"But what if it's not?" asked Jay. "What if Zane's alive?!"

"The Tournament of Elements," said Lloyd. "I think Master Chen makes more than noodles."

Kai agreed. "Forget about bringing in a new ninja, Lloyd. Let's go see about an old friend!"

A SECRET MISSION

That night, Lloyd packed a bag. "The guys and I are going fishing," he told Garmadon.

"Good to hear the team's back together," Garmadon replied.

"Dad," said Lloyd, "are there others out there with elemental powers like ours?"

"Why would you ask?" replied his father.

"No reason," said Lloyd. "See ya."

At midnight, the ninja gathered on the dock. They were not alone. Many others were waiting for the boat to Chen's island.

"You think all these people have powers like us?" asked Kai.

"When I asked my dad about it, he acted funny," said Lloyd. "Like he's keeping something from me."

As the ninja waited, they watched the other passengers.

"We don't know yet if this is a trap," said Lloyd. "Wherever they take us, we have to stick together. We can't let anything distract us. You hear me, Kai?"

But Kai was distracted by a beautiful woman stepping onto the boat. "Yeah," Kai agreed. "Whatever you said."

"Master Chen will be charmed to see the ninja," said Chen's right-hand man, Clouse. "A Master of Spinjitzu shall fare well in his tournament."

"We're not here to fight," said Jay. "We're here to save a friend."

Clouse smiled. "Everyone here has something to fight for, Master Jay." He reached into Jay's bag and took out his nunchuks.

Jay grinned. "They're chopsticks. I'm a big eater."

Suddenly, Garmadon ran down the dock. He had followed the ninja!

"Lloyd—wait! If you get on that boat, you may never return. Whatever Master Chen promised you, do not believe him."

Clouse stepped forward. "Lord Garmadon. It's been a while."

Garmadon narrowed his eyes. "Clouse. I see Master Chen still has you running his errands."

AN UNINVITED GUEST

"I have to go, Dad," said Lloyd. "This is about Zane. It's about family."

"I can't stop you, son. But I can join you," Garmadon said.

"Sorry, no more room," said Clouse.

Garmadon leaped on board, pushing one of Chen's guys overboard.

Clouse shrugged. "I stand corrected. There's room now."

As the steamboat sailed through the night, Kai watched the other passengers practice their powers. "Why haven't you or Wu ever told us there are others with powers like us?"

"Because," said Garmadon, "there are some things we didn't want you to know."

THE ELEMENTAL MASTERS

"Everyone on this ship is a descendant of an original elemental master," explained Garmadon.

"Elemental masters?" asked Lloyd. "Who were they?"

"They were the First Spinjitzu Master's guardians," said Garmadon. "Each has an elemental power that has passed down through generations. For instance, that pale man is a relative of the Master of Light."

"Then there's Griffin Turner, grandson to the Master of Speed."

"And who's she?" wondered Kai, pointing to the woman he'd seen earlier.

Garmadon shrugged. "I don't know most of these people . . . but they will all be gunning for you. You are ninja. You serve with honor. Here, that means very little."

"Well, maybe honor means something to me," Kai said. A huge man was arguing with the woman. Kai went over to defend her.

"It's okay. I can handle myself," the woman told him.

"This is none of his business," the big man said. "Karlof cold. Karlof want her cloak."

"You look like you've got big enough mittens already," Kai said.

"These not mittens," shouted Karlof. "These crush ninja."

Kai laughed. "I'd like to see you try."

"Don't think Karlof afraid of you," the big guy growled.

"No, you don't think much at all, do you?" Kai said.

"Save it for the tournament, Kai," Garmadon warned.

But Kai's fiery temper got the better of him. He stepped forward, ready to fight!

Karlof was tougher than he looked. He slammed his fists together, and his whole body turned to metal!

Kai attacked Karlof. But every time he landed a blow, Karlof just seemed to get stronger.

"We should help him," Lloyd said.

"You can help him by staying out of it," said Garmadon. "Sooner or later, you must fight your own battles. You can't all win the tournament."

“Enough!” Clouse shouted. “We’re here. Welcome to Chen’s island.”

The two fighters stepped away from each other. Everyone stared at the huge island looming in the mist.

“I swore never to return,” Garmadon muttered.

“If Zane’s on that island, we’ll find him. We have to,” Lloyd declared.

As the boat approached shore, Clouse called Master Chen. "Garmadon has returned."

"Interesting," said Chen. He peered into a prison cell. A familiar ninja lay within: Zane!

Master Chen laughed. "You worry too much, Clouse. Just wait and see. I hold all the cards."